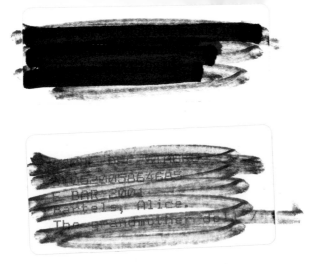

101

The GRANDMOTHER DOLL

Story by
Alice L. Bartels

Illustrated by
Dušan Petričić

ANNICK PRESS LTD.
TORONTO ◆ NEW YORK ◆ VANCOUVER

Katy was having one of those days.

So was Katy's mother.

"Please turn off the TV," she told Katy.

"Now!"

Katy turned off the TV with a snap.

She stomped into her bedroom.
She slammed the door.

Hard.

The sun was pouring in her window, but Katy had
to stay indoors. She had the flu, and she was hot, achy,
and angry.

"It's not fair," she told herself out loud. "I almost
never get to watch TV!"

"At least you have a TV," a small voice said, "which
is more than some people do."

"Who's that?" asked Katy. "Who's there?"

"I'm here," the voice replied.

Katy looked. She could only see the Grandmother Doll that had belonged to her mother many years ago.

"Is that you?" Katy asked. "Talking? I didn't know you could talk."

"I can talk. I can hear and I can see, too," the Grandmother Doll informed her. "But I can't watch TV because I don't have a TV.

Not that I'm complaining."

Katy thought.

"Maybe I can make you a TV," she said after a while. Katy went to her junk box and found the things she needed.

Here is what she found:

A small box

A pair of scissors

Some crayons

A piece of paper

Sticky tape

Katy cut a large hole in one side of the box. She used the crayon to draw knobs under the hole. Then she drew a picture of a talking man on the piece of paper. She taped it inside the box. When it was ready she put it beside the Grandmother Doll.

"Well," sniffed the Grandmother Doll. "That's certainly a boring program."

She stood up and walked to the TV. She turned the knobs and a monster appeared on the screen.

It was chasing some people through a city and
knocking over the tall buildings.

"That's better," the Grandmother Doll remarked,
and sat down again. The Grandmother Doll and Katy
watched until the end.

Katy was still having one of those days.
So was Katy's mother.

"Please stop eating those cookies," she
told Katy.

"Now!"

Katy stomped into her bedroom.
She slammed the door.

Hard.

"I'm hungry," she told herself out loud. "In fact, I'm starving! I've had hardly any of the cookies!"

"At least you've had some cookies," the Grandmother Doll said, "which is more than some people did."

Katy looked at her.

"Can you eat cookies?" she asked.

"I could eat cookies," the Grandmother Doll told her, "if I had some cookies. And I could make some cookies if I had a stove to cook with.

Not that I'm complaining."

Katy thought.

"I made you a TV," Katy said. "Maybe I can make you a stove."

Katy went to her junk box and found what she needed.

Here is what she found:

A small box

   A crayon

She drew some burners on top of the box. Then she drew an oven door on the front, and knobs to turn on the burners, and a big knob for the oven.

When it was ready, she put it beside the Grandmother Doll.

The Grandmother Doll put down her knitting
and went to the stove. She opened the oven door.
A delicious smell floated out. She pulled out a pan
of tiny chocolate cookies.

"A little over-done," she told Katy. "Because you
took so long."

She offered Katy the pan of cookies.

As soon as Katy took one of the tiny cookies, it grew into an extra-big cookie that tasted exactly like the ones her mother always made.

The Grandmother Doll put the tray of cookies beside her chair and turned on her TV. There was a show about a giant spider.

Katy and the Grandmother Doll watched until the end and ate every one of the cookies.

Supper was over and it was getting late.
Katy's mother was glad this day would
soon be over.

Katy wasn't.

"It's time to go to bed,"
Katy's mother said.

"Now!"

Katy stomped into her bedroom. She
slammed the door. Hard.

"I won't go to bed," she said to herself out
loud. "I was in bed all day yesterday and the day
before. I hate bed!"

"At least you have a bed," the Grandmother
Doll said. "Which is more than some people do."

"Can you sleep?" Katy asked.

"I can sleep. Sometimes I sleep in my chair. It
must be nice to sleep in a bed," the Grandmother
Doll continued. "Not that I'm complaining."

Katy thought.

"I have made you a TV and a stove," Katy said. "A bed should be easy to make."

Katy went to her junk box and found the things she needed. Here is what she found:

A small box

A pair of scissors

Some scraps of fabric

Katy folded a piece of fabric and put it inside the box to make it soft. Then she folded another piece for a pillow.

"I'll have that one for my blanket," the Grandmother Doll told Katy.

Katy cut the pink and blue piece so that it would be the right size for a cover.

When it was finished, Katy put the bed beside the Grandmother Doll.

The Grandmother Doll stood up and stretched.

Then she yawned.

"It's past my bedtime," she said. She took off her glasses. Then she climbed into her bed and pulled the cover up to her nose.

"Good night," she said.

Katy climbed into her own bed and closed her eyes.

Maybe tomorrow the Grandmother Doll would make some brownies in the stove. And maybe they could watch a movie about robots or spaceships on the TV. Maybe she should make a bigger TV...

When Katy's mother came in to say good night, Katy was already asleep.

Her mother saw the little TV, and she
could smell the chocolate cookies. Then
she walked to the Grandmother Doll's
new bed. She tucked in the blanket.
"At it again?" Katy's mother
whispered softly.

For Natasha and Jessica, and for Dennis
—A.B.

For Misha
—D.P.

Annick Press Ltd.
All rights reserved. No part of this work covered by the copyrights hereon may be reproduced or used in any form or by any means – graphic, electronic, or mechanical – without the prior written permission of the publisher.

We acknowledge the support of the Canada Council for the Arts, the Ontario Arts Council, and the Government of Canada through the Book Publishing Industry Development Program (BPIDP) for our publishing activities.

Cataloging in Publication Data
        Bartels, Alice
                The grandmother doll

Rev. ed.
ISBN 1-55037-667-5 (bound)   ISBN 1-55037-666-7 (pbk.)

I. Petričić, Dušan. II. Title.

PS8553.A77176G73 2001   jC813'.54 C00-932607-3
PZ7.B37Gr 2001

The art in this book was rendered in watercolors.
The text was typeset in Jenson.

Distributed in Canada by: Published in the U.S.A. by Annick Press (U.S.) Ltd.
Firefly Books Ltd.   Distributed in the U.S.A. by:
3680 Victoria Park Avenue   Firefly Books (U.S.) Inc.
Willowdale, ON   P.O. Box 1338
M2H 3K1   Ellicott Station
                                 Buffalo, NY 14205

Printed and bound in Canada by Friesens, Altona, Manitoba.

visit us at: **www.annickpress.com**